ELLA
Diaries

TOP SECRET!

Meredith Costain

For Sadie and Jade—who love sewing!—M.C.

For my sister, Jo. It's never too late to follow your 'passion for fashion'.—D.M.

Danielle McDonald

Scholastic Australia
An imprint of Scholastic Australia Pty Limited
PO Box 579 Gosford NSW 2250
ABN 11 000 614 577
www.scholastic.com.au

Part of the Scholastic Group
Sydney · Auckland · New York · Toronto · London · Mexico City
· New Delhi · Hong Kong · Buenos Aires · Puerto Rico

Published by Scholastic Australia in 2020.
Text copyright © Meredith Costain, 2020.
Illustrations copyright © Danielle McDonald, 2020.

Meredith Costain asserts her moral rights as the author of this work.
Danielle McDonald asserts her moral rights as the illustrator of this work.

 A catalogue record for this book is available from the National Library of Australia

ISBN: 978-1-74383-231-8

Typeset in Sweetie Pie.

Printed in China by Hang Tai Printing Company Limited.

Scholastic Australia's policy, in association with Hang Tai, is to use papers that are renewable and made efficiently from wood grown in responsibly managed forests, so as to minimise its environmental footprint.

10 9 8 7 6 5 4 3 2 1   20 21 22 23 24 / 2

ELLA
Diaries

PASSION FOR FASHION

Friday night, after dinner

Dear Diary,

I am sooooo exciterated!

Our school is having a disco NEXT WEEK!

I ♥ school discos. You get to dress up in really cool outfits, and do your hair in super-stylish ways. You even get to put disco make-up on!

OLIVIA

ME

Glittery

EYESHADOW

STRAWBERRY-FLAVOURED LIP BALM

ZOE

ME

Last year, Zoe (my best BFF) won a prize for CRAZIEST DISCO HAIR. Even though she was only in Grade Four back then! Her cousin Nella, who is sixteen and knows EVERYTHING about hair, did it for her. It took the WHOLE afternoon.

HAIR FOUNTAIN

GLITTER BOW

BRAIDS

ZOE

Head BAND

CRAZIEST DISCO HAIR!

And Georgia—who is one of my second-best friends—won a prize for BEST DISCO DANCING.

GEORGIA

BEST Disco Dancing

Every year there is a different theme.

Last year we
all dressed up
as creatures
and machines
from outer
space.

And the year
before that we
had a circus
theme.

But guess what the theme is going to be this year?????

You never will in a pazillion years so I'll just tell you.

We all have to get dressed up as something beginning with P!

YESSSSS!!

This year's theme is PERFECT for me!

I have so many magnificently marvellous and excellent ideas for sensationally stylish outfits.

And then I had the most excellentest idea of all. It is something that nobody else in the whole entire school would ever even think of. Even if they spent a pazillion to the power of a bazillion years thinking up ideas for outfits beginning with P.

And guess what it is?

I am going to go as a . . .

Wait for it . . .

Here it comes . . .

A pangolin!

Pangolins are my third favourite animal at the moment, after dogs and whales. I've been making a **FACT♥FILE** all about them for a book I am writing called *Ella's Big Book of Favourite Animals*.

FACT
FILE

Pangolins are aMAZing. And also Excellent.
And fanTABulously fabulous!

They have super-scaly bodies and teensy-
tiny little head parts. And also a really,
really, REALLY long, pink flicky tongue
they use to slurp up ants with.

Like this:

PANGOLIN

SLUUURRRPPP!

PANGOLIN'S
TONGUE

ANT

And if they get scared by something, they just roll up into a ball so the scary thing can't tell they are even an animal anymore. Hehehe. They look just like a big round spikerous pine cone.

HEY! WHERE DID it GO?

SCARY THING

PHEW.

ROLLED-UP PANGOLIN

And they have sweet little babies that they carry around on their tail part.

Like this:

Mama PANGOLIN

BABY Pangolin

TaiL PART

I'm going to start making my pangolin costume tomorrow. I might even make a baby pangolin one as well✳.

✳ I just had ANOTHER marvellously magnificent and excellent idea. Maybe Zoe could dress up as my baby! We could do a double act again, like we did at the circus disco, when we went as a horse and rider.

I can't wait until tomorrow so I can tell Zoe all about it!

Love,
Ella
XOXO

Saturday, before dinner

Dear Diary,

I rang Zoe FIRST THING this morning to tell her I'd had a brilliant idea for my disco costume. And also to find out if she wanted to come over to my place to help me make it. And maybe even be part of it!!

And guess what?

Zoe said she'd also had a brilliant idea last night. She's going to dress up as a puppet!

But not the type of puppet that people put on their hand or finger parts.

HAND PUPPET

FINGER PUPPET

She's going to be one of those special puppets with strings joined onto their arm and leg parts that make them dance and move around. The type that has golden ringlets and long spiky eyelashes and sweet little outfits with lots of frills and bows on them.

And she wants ME to be the puppeteer, to move her strings up and down so she can dance.

Being a puppeteer sounds B-O-R-I-N-G with a capital B. The puppet is the one who gets to have all the fun dancing around. And what are you even supposed to wear?

PUPPETEER

BORING OUTFIT

CONTROL BAR

PUPPET

STRINGS

sweet LITTLE OUTFIT

So I said thanks, but no thanks.

So I spent the WHOLE DAY making a pangolin costume all by myself.

It is going to be aMAZing!

Yours truly,
Ella
XOXO

Sunday night, after dinner

Dear Diary,

Zoe and Ammy came over today to show me their puppet and puppeteer costumes. Ammy's step-mum helped them too.

Zoe even did a little dance for me in her outfit.

They looked aMAZing!

Ammy's puppeteer outfit wasn't boring at all.

Zoe said it wasn't too late for me to change my mind about my outfit for the disco. She said I could be a puppet too if I wanted. We could even do a puppet dance together!

Doing a puppet dance with Zoe sounded like fun. Especially if I also put GOLDEN RINGLETS on my head part and got to wear one of those sweet little frilly costumes.

But I've already started making my pangolin costume. So I said no.

I just need a bit more time to make it all work. ☹

E

Monday, after school

Dearest Diary,

Everyone was talking about their outfits for the disco at school today!

Georgia and Poppy and Chloe and Daisy are all going as pieces of pizza (with pineapple).

Pineapple

PINEAPPLE ON PIZZA?

BLEUCHHH.

Peter and Raf and George are going as police officers eating packets of popcorn.

Cordelia is going as a PHARAOH.

My annoying little sister Olivia and her BFFs Matilda and Bethany are going as the Three Little Pigs. (Ha!)

OINK!

And Precious Princess Peach Parker is going as herself✳.

✳ ~~Acksh~~ Actually, she's going as 'Celebrity Peach', the character she played in the vlog she made for our **SHINE** project.

Prinny is going as her photographer. And Jade is going to be her poodle. ☺

PRINNY CELEBRITY PEACH JADE

Seven people in my class are going as pirates. And six are going to be princesses. (I did a survey.)

🍍	PineAPPLe	1
🐼	PANDA	2
☠	Pirate	7
👑	PRiNCess	6
🍕	PiZZA	4

But *nobody* else is going as a pangolin. I just need to do a few more things and my costume will be all ready to go.

Actually, I need to do a LOT more things.
I can't seem to get it to work the way I
want . . . ☹

Ella

X

Tuesday, after school

still not working . . .

Wednesday, after dinner

STILL not working . . .

Thursday, after dinner

I am in DESPERATING DESPAIR.
Why didn't I just decide to be a
pirate? Or a princess?
Or a . . . a pumpkin. ☹

The disco is in
two more days
and I STILL don't
have my costume
ready for it.

Maybe I'll just
stay home instead.
☹☹☹

About half an hour later . . .

Dear Diary,

Here is a heartfelt and sensitive poem I wrote about my disco costume dilemma.

It's called 'The Problem with Pangolins'.

Pangolin, pangolin,
Covered with scales
I can't make this work
And it's making me wail!

Pangolin—I thought
You'd make a good friend
But your costume's a mess—
I just want this to end . . . ☹

Friday, very late, in bed

Dearest Diary,

You will never EVER guess what happened
tonight!!! It was SOOOO AMAZING!

Mum and Dad went to an importerant meeting at Mum's work.

But that's not the aMAZing thing. The aMAZing thing is the thing that happened when Nanna Kate came over to look after me and Olivia and Max.

We had spaghetti bolognese for dinner! My favourite!

SLURP!

But *that's* not the aMAZing thing either.

The aMAZing thing is WHAT HAPPENED when Nanna Kate came into my room to have a nice chat. And she saw bits of my pangolin costume all over the floor.

Here's what we said.

Nanna Kate (kindly): What
are you making, sweetheart?
A giant jigsaw puzzle?
Me (sadly): No.
Nanna Kate: A dog coat for Bob?
Me (even more sadly): No.
Nanna Kate: I know! A lampshade?
Me (even sadder than that): It's a
pangolin costume.
Nanna Kate: A what?
Me: A pangolin costume.
For the school disco
tomorrow afternoon. We have to go as
something starting with P.

Nanna Kate: Of course it is! Silly me. It's a lovely one too. Look at these sweet little . . . umm . . . legs.

Me (so sad I am thinking about rolling myself up into a pangolin-shaped ball and then rolling away under the bed, never to be seen again): It isn't lovely at all. It doesn't even LOOK like a pangolin. It's just a big, giganterous mess. ☹☹☹

And then guess what Nanna Kate did next?

She went out into the hallway and opened up the VERY TOPPEST TOP hallway cupboard. And guess what was in there?

Mum's old sewing machine! Nanna Kate said it would be PERFECT for making a pangolin costume.

So we did.

Nanna Kate had LOTS of excellent ideas for my costume.

First of all we found some of Dad's old T-shirts in our Rag Bag. Our Rag Bag is chock full of all kinds of useful stuff for craft and gardening projects.

Nanna Kate and I cut up an orange one and a brown one to make new scales for my costume. Olivia helped a bit. (And also Max and Bob.)

GRRRR!

Then Nanna Kate and I did A BIG SEARCH through all my bedroom drawers to find something to sew them onto.

Look what we found!
My old onesie!

Nanna Kate showed
me how to use
Mum's sewing
machine to sew the
scales.

It was a bit tricky to
start off with. So
tricky I had to have
a few goes before
I got it all working
properly.

But sewing bits together with a sewing machine is SUPER FAST. And also EASY-PEASY! (Mostly. ☺) And then we made an extra loooooooooooooong tongue out of my dressing gown cord.

Now my pangolin costume looks like this!

ME

MY PANGOLIN COSTUME

Hehehe. It's so EXCITERATING, Diary!
Looks like I CAN go to the disco after all!

Yours 4 ever,
Ella
XOXO

Saturday night, in bed

Dear Diary-doo,

The disco was aMAZing! And
excellent! And fantabulously
fabulous! They played ALL our
favourite Cassi Valentine* songs!

Cassi Valentine

✳ Cassi Valentine is the most excellent pop music singer in the history of pop music singers. And also my NOMFS (Number One Most Favouritest Singer) in the whole wild world. All the girls in my class ♥ her too.

ZOE AND AMMY AND I DANCED THE WHOLE TIME!

And so did Poppy and Chloe and Georgia and Daisy. Except for when all their pineapple bits fell off. They had to crawl around on the floor on their hand and knee parts looking for them so they didn't get squasherated by dancing pelicans and palm trees. (The pineapple pieces. Not Poppy and Chloe and Georgia and Daisy.)

Even Peach and Prinny and Jade looked like they were having a good time. (Mostly.)

CLICK CLICK!

JADE

YaP! YaP!

PRINNY

PeacH

There was just one BIG PROBLEM.

The decorations this year were B-O-R-I-N-G with a capital B.

They weren't even any TWINKLY LIGHTS.

Or sparkly streamers.

Or disco balls with sweet little mirrors on them hanging from the ceiling.

Just giganterous letter Ps everywhere.

Like this.

Zoe and Ammy and I were SHOCKED.

Last year, the decorations for the outer space theme looked AMAZING!

That's because all the Grade Six students on last year's DDC✳ were exCEPtionally stylish. And also creativerous to the power of eleven.

✳ DDC stands for Disco Decorations Committee✳✳.

✳✳ Being on the DDC next year is one of my mainerest ambitions. (After saving the planet and making all the endangered animals unendangered again.) I have been wanting to be a ~~DISCO~~ DECORATOR ever since my first school disco, way, way back in ~~ainsh~~ ancient times when I was in Grade One.

ME

ZOE

PEACH PARKER

(BEFORE the GIGANTEROUS ~~FIGHT~~ ~~ARGUMENT~~ TERRIBLE thing SHE DID WHICH CHANGED OUR LIVES FOREVER)

I CAN'T WAIT until next year so I can be a  Decorator and show everyone my exceptionally stylish ideas!

Love,
Ella
XOXO

Sunday evening, before dinner

Dear Diary,

I was a teensy bit tired this morning after our big day at the disco.

So I had a nice relaxing rest on the couch, looking at ALL THE PICTURES Cordelia took of our class.

My pangolin outfit looked senSATional! And making it had been funnerous fun! So much fun I decided I needed to use Mum's old sewing machine again to make something else. Straightaway right then!

So I called Nanna Kate and she came over to help me use the machine.

Here are some of the things we made:

1. A superhero mask for Max, for when
he's old enough to go to the school disco.
Max ♥s superheroes!

We made a mask shape out of cardboard.
Then we cut up some old towels and two
bits of red ribbon (so we could tie his
mask at the back) and glued them over the
top of it.

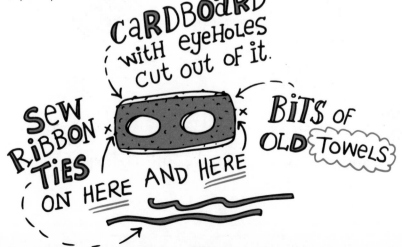

CARDBOARD
with eyeHoLes
cut out of it.

SEW
RiBBON
TiES
ON HERE AND HERE

BiTS OF
OLD TOWELS

And also a specTACularly stylish cape for Max to casually fling around his shoulders, superhero-style.

KNOT tHe ENDS togetHeR HERE.

CUT SHaPeS OUT HERE.

2 A stylish new nightie for Olivia, out of another one of Dad's old T-shirts.

This one has really cool rockets on it! Olivia ♥s rockets. She's building one in her bedroom at the moment. (And also a time machine. Though I'm not absolutely 100 per cent sure this part is true.)

It was also easy-peasy to make. I used the sewing machine to sew some new seams down each side, to make it less widerous.

WHIRRRRRRrrrr.

And then Nanna Kate showed me how to unpick the start of the seam around the neck and sleeve parts so we could thread some elastic through. It fit her much betterer after we did that!

ELASTIC Goes HERE.

NEW seams→

DAD'S OLD T-SHIRT

TA-DAA!

This is what Olivia's new nightie looks like! She s it too!

BEFORE   AFTER

But the absolutely, totally, best thing we made today was

Sorry, Diary, I have to stop writing now. Olivia✳ just banged REALLY LOUDLY on my door SIX TIMES to let me know that dinner is ready.

I'll write more as soon as I get back, I promise!

Ella

Sunday night, after dinner

Dear Diary,

I'm back! Guess what Max wore to dinner???

Hehehe. I don't think Max ever wants to take his mask off.

He couldn't see his food properly so it kept falling off his fork. Especially the broccoli bits.

Broccoli. BLEUCHHH.

(Bob was SUPER happy though. ☺)

Anyway, the absolutely, totally, BESTEREST thing we made today was . . .

witches' BRitcHeS!!!

Nanna Kate said she used to wear them under her school uniform to keep her legs warm, way back in the Dark Ages about 900 years ago.

"FREEZEROUS"
WINTER SCHOOL UNIFORMS
BACK IN THE DARK Ages.

Back then, at her school, all the girls had to wear super-thin dresses called tunics in winter.

No comfy, warm school-uniform pants like WE get to wear. ☺

COMFY AND **WARM**
WINTER SCHOOL
UNIFORMS today.

Making witches' britches was easy-peasy to the power of a pazillion.

We found some lacy ribbons in an ~~anch~~ ancient old tin right at the back of the same cupboard the sewing machine was in.

Zow-ie! The words on the tin look like my mum's handwriting! The secret sewing stuff must be hers! Who even knew?!!!

EVEN **MORE** DUST.

MY BIG TIN OF SEWING STUFF. KEEP OUT!

EWW

We sewed three rows of pink lacy ribbon to the bottom parts of my second-best bike shorts. Now they look like this:

SECOND-BeSt BiKe SHORTS

LACY RIBBON

I'm going to wear them to school tomorrow.

Everyone is going to love them for sure!

Good night
Sleep tight
Don't let
The dust bugs
BITE!

(Or make you sneeze. ☺)

Ella xx

Monday, after school

Dear Diary,

I wore my witches' britches to school today! Except I've decided to call them 'sporty shorties' instead. ☺

It took AGES AND AGES AND AGES for anyone to even notice I was wearing them. ☹

So I waited until
Zoe and Ammy
(and also a few
of my second-best
friends like Poppy
and Georgia and Chloe
and Daisy) were all
in the same part of
the playground✱ at
lunchtime.

ZOE

Ammy ♥

POPPY

GeoRGia

ChLoe

DaiSy

✱ The back part near the big
trees behind the basketball
courts where the boys NEVER EVER go.
(Boys. BLeuCHHH.)

And then I casually did a whole lot of
cartwheels in a row in front of them.

This is what everyone said next:

And then a whole lot of other girls from my class (and also some I have never even met before) came rushing over like RUSHING WINDS to see what was going on.

And they all thought my witches' britches were really cool and amazing as well!

So then I told everyone that my witches' britches weren't ~~acksh~~ actually bike shorts. They were a brand new and extremely stylish fashion item called sporty shorties that you wear underneath your dress to keep your leg parts warm. And all the main importerant people (and also models) in the top fashion places, like Paris in France, had at least three pairs✱.

✱ This part might be a teensy-tiny bit made-up. ☺

And also that I'd made them ALL BY MYSELF (with a little bit of help from my nanna).

This is what they said back:

There were so many sporty shortie-
wantering girls crowding around me I was
in grave and also mortal danger of getting
squasherated.

I was just starting to open up my mouth really, really wide so I could do a giganterous scream for Zoe and Ammy to help save me when . . .

DOOT! DOOT! DOOT!

the bell went for the end of lunchtime.

PHEW!

All my second-best friends and the other girls suddenly stopped crowding around me and ran off to line up outside their classrooms, ready to go back in.

Zoe and Ammy both gave me nice comforting pats on my arm parts, to make sure I was OK and not too overwhelmed✳ by all the sporty shorties fans.

✳ 'Overwhelmed' is my new favourite word at the moment. It means how you feel when there are too many things crowding in on top of you all at the same time.

OVERWHELMED

★ DEALING with ANNOYING sister

★ HOMeWORK

★ PLAYiNG with My FRieNds

★ BEiNG excellent at EVERYTHING

★ saving the planet

★ Running emergency MeeTiNGS

It does NOT mean a long warm jacket thing you wear over the top of your other clothes on freezerous cold and/or rainy days. That is an overcoat.

OVERCOAT

Then we had a nice long chat, even though the bell had already dooted and it was time for us to rush off to class with everyone else.

This is what we all said.

Zoe (admiringly): Those sporty shorties are aMAZing! And also excellent. Did you REALLY make them?
Me (proudly): Yep.
Ammy (suspiciously): REALLY TRULY?
Me: Yep.
Ammy (even more suspiciously): I didn't even know you knew how to sew.

Me: Nanna Kate showed me yesterday. It was funnerous fun!

Zoe (impressed): Wow.

Ammy (even more impressed): Double wow.

Me: ☺

Ammy: Did you make anything else?

So then I told them all about the superhero mask and cape I made for Max out of bits of old towel. And also the sensationally-stylish rocket nightie I casually threw together for Olivia out of one of Dad's old T-shirts.

Then Zoe looked at me with SHINY EYES. So shiny I could see Mrs Sneed (the assistant principal) marching across the playground to find out why we weren't rushing rushingly off to class with everyone else reflected in them.

MRS SNEED

And guess what she said next? (Zoe, not Mrs Sneed.)

I've just had a BRILLIANT IDEA!

Have to go now, Diary! Zoe and Ammy are turning up any moment for an SSEM* here in my bedroom so we can discuss Zoe's brilliant idea! And I haven't even started organisering the snacks yet!

* SSEM stands for Sporty Shorties Emergency Meeting.

Yours 4 ever (and ever),
Ella
xx

Monday night, very late, in bed

Dearest Diary,

We had our SSEM. And it was **AMAZING!** And **EXCELLENT!** And fantabulously **fABULOUS!**

I didn't need to put up a KEEP OUT THIS MEANS YOU OLIVIA!! sign on my door or black out my windows this time, because Olivia was over at her BFF Matilda's place, doing whatever annoying little sisters do when they're visiting their best friends.

OLIVIA

MATILDA

TOP THREE THINGS THAT ANNOYING LITTLE SISTERS (PROBABLY) DO WHEN VISITING THEIR FRIENDS

① Have a fairy tea party with make-believe fairy guests and baby dollies and little teacups and saucers and fakerous fairy cakes.

Make-Believe Fairy guests

Matilda

OLIVIA

BABY DOLLY

FAKEROUS FAIRY CAKES

2 Annoy their friend's brothers and/or sisters as much as they annoy me by sneaking into their room and going through all their stuff.

3 Set up a long-range ~~survalance~~ ~~survaylance~~ surveillance system so they can still spy on my Emergency Meeting, even though THEY ARE NOT EVEN AT OUR HOUSE!!! ☹

MY BEDROOM WINDOW

EXTReMeLY POWERFUL SUPERSONIC BiNOCULARS that let you HEAR other people's SECRET conversations as well as SEE them

OLiVia's BFF MATiLDA

OLiVia

MATiLDA'S BACKYARD

First of all we ate
all the snacks.

Then we got down
to the importerant business.

And guess what it is?! You never will in a
pazillion gazillion years, even though I left
you a VIC (Very Importerant Clue) a few
sentences ago. So I'll just tell you.

HINT (in case you want to try to work it out before I tell you): The sentence with the VIC in it begins like this: 'Then we got down to the . . .'

STILL can't guess it????

OK, here it comes.

Zoe thinks we should set up our own BUSINESS. All about sewing!

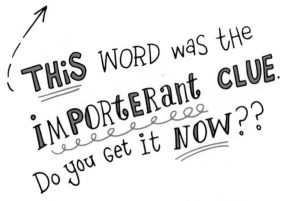

THiS WORD waS tHe IMPORtERant CLUE. Do you Get it NOW??

She thinks that my sporty shorties are obviously *soooo popular* we could probably sell a pazillion pairs in ONE DAY! And also some stylish nighties and superhero mask and cape sets. Maybe even some pangolin outfits, in case anyone was going to a wildlife fancy-dress dress-up party.

SUPERHERO MASK aND cape SETS

SPORTY SHORTIES

Pangolin outfits

STYLISH NiGHTies

This is what we all said next.

Me: Wow, Zoe. Your
brilliant idea is
BRILLIANT!
Zoe: I know.
Ammy: Everyone
is going to want
a pair for sure.

Me: Maybe even TWO pairs!
Ammy: We are going to

make sooooo much money.
Zoe: I know. Heaps and heaps of lovely money.
Probably enough to buy my own horse.
Me: Or even TWO horses.
Zoe: For sure.

I was just about to ask Zoe what type of horses she was going to get when Ammy came up with an importerant point.

We needed a name for our business. One that was clever. And also super easy to remember.

So we brainstormed✳ some good ideas for it on a giganterous sheet of paper.

✳ Brainstorming means jotting down all the ideas that breeze into your brain until you come up with something really excellent and/or amazing.

It does NOT mean a storm inside your brain. That would just be WEIRD.

Here are the toppest of the top name ideas
we came up with:

Name	Whose idea?	Comments
CRafty GiRLS	Ella	This was Zoe's favourite
SEWING 'R' US	Ammy	BLEUCHHH!
SEW WHat?	Ella	This was Ammy's favourite

★Super★ ★Sewing★ ★Stars★	Zoe	B-O-R-I-N-G (This is the kind of name Olivia would come up with)
EZA Sewing Services (EZA stands for Ella, Zoe and Ammy)	Ammy	Even MORE B-O-R-I-N-G
RAG BAGS	Zoe	DOUBLE BLEUCHHH!
Rags②Riches	Ammy	My favourite
Witches' Stitches	Ella	My second favourite

And guess which one we all picked as the besterest one?

RAGS 2 RICHES is the PERFECT name for us!

I was just doodling some little doodles
of what our logo could look like and
dreaming about all the FANTABULOUSLY
FABULOUS things I was going to buy with
all our riches when . . .

Da Da Da... DUMMmm.

I had a whole heap of
horrifically horrendous
thoughts. So horrifically
horrendous I was too scared
to say them out
loud in case that made them real.

I must have looked SUPER horrified on the outside as well as also feeling that way on the inside, because Zoe gave me a worried look. The kind of look Mum gives Max when he comes back inside from playing dinosaurs out in the backyard and has a giganterous bump on his knee part.

GIGANTEROUS BUMP

KNEE PART

Max

And then all the horrifyingly horrendous thoughts SWIRLING AROUND AND AROUND inside my brain came gushing out, the way water rushes down the gutter in a giganterous thunderstorm.

Like this:

HORRIFYINGLY HORRENDOUS THOUGHT NUMBER ①

Where are we going to get all the second-best bike shorts and old (extra-extra-large) T-shirts and ribbony bits from?

HORRIFYINGLY HORRENDOUS
THOUGHT NUMBER 2

Where are we going to keep all the extra
sewing machines we'll need to make everything
on? (And what if we have to keep them all
in my bedroom which means—HORROR OF
HORRORS—I will have to move in with Olivia,
NOOOOOOOO!

HORRIFYINGLY HORRENDOUS THOUGHT NUMBER ③

What if everyone decides they don't ~~acksh~~ actually like our stuff after all and we are stuck with A PAZILLION AND SIX pairs of sporty shorties? (And also stylish nighties and pangolin costumes and superhero mask and cape sets.)

Zoe and Ammy were SHOCKED.

But then, after a bit, they stopped being shocked, and said comforting things like this:

And then we made a ~~moo-chewal~~ mutual
decision* to totally abandon the whole idea.

* A mutual decision is when everyone in
the group agrees to do something. It has
got NOTHING WHATSOEVER to do with
cows. Or mooing. Or chewing.

It's so not fair, Diary. I really, really, REALLY wanted to have a sewing business called Rags 2 Riches. EsPECially the Riches part. ☹☹☹

We all just sat there and stared out the window in deeperous dejection for a while, dreaming of what might have been.

And then, all of a suddenly, SHINY EYES Zoe's eyes went all shiny. As shiny as the sewing needles on Mum's (dusted) sewing machine.

Zoe

Zoe (exciteredly): I've just had ANOTHER brilliant idea!

Ammy: Do we have to guess what it is?

Zoe: Yep.

Me: We ask a famous sewing machine company to donate a pazillion sewing machines to our school? And then we can still do **Rags 2 Riches** but I won't have to share a bedroom with Olivia?

Zoe: Nope. Guess again.

Ammy: We write to Cassi Valentine and ask her to wear Ella's sporty shorties in her next music video so that all her biggest fans see them and want some too?

SPORTY SHORTIES

Cassi Valentine

Zoe: Nope. Guess again.

Me: Your mum knows a famous supermodel in Paris in France who has offered to model my sporty shorties on catwalks around the world?

Zoe: Nope. But close!

(CLOSE?!?! Zow-ie. I NEVER get close!!)

So then I had to know what the brilliant idea was imMEDiately straightaway right then!

And guess what it is?

Zoe thinks we should set up a Lunchtime School Sewing Club! (LSSC for short.)
At lunchtimes! And invite other people to join it!

And we could ask Ms Kahlo (our exceptionally arty and crafty art and craft teacher) if she can help us do the sewing! And also unlock the locked cupboard where the school sewing machines* are kept.

* I didn't even know we had ANY sewing machines at our school. But Zoe told us just now there are three of them in there. THREE!? Who even knew?

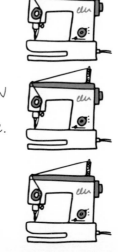

SEWING MACHINES LIVE IN **HERE**

LOCKED CUPBOARD

ZOE

MS KAHLO

And people could bring in their OWN second-best bike shorts or old extra-extra-large T-shirts and ribbony bits so we didn't have to. Or any other bits they want to use.

And we could have an LSSC Committee and be the main importerant people in charge of all the sewing!

So we closed down our Sporty Shorties Committee Emergency Meeting and held a new, improved LSSC Committee Emergency Meeting instead.

The first thing we did was get some more snacks from the kitchen.

Then I gave everyone some big sheets of cardboard and coloured marker pens from my Big Box of Craft Supplies and we made some artistical posters to put up at school.

Do you LOVE MAKING stuff? ☐

Have you got a RAG BAG or WARDROBE at HOME CHOCK-FULL OF OLD CLOTHES nobody wears anymore? ☐

ARE you EXCEPTIONALLY creativerous? ☐

OR STYLISHLY FASHIONABLE? ☐

OR BOTH? ☐

Do you ever get BORED at LUNCHTIME Because there is NOTHING even Remotely exciterating to Do? ☐

If you ticked three or MORE Boxes come to the ART AND CRAFT ROOM at 1.15 p.m. SHARP Today AND FIND OUT ALL about How to join our FANTABULOUSLY AMAZING LSSC*!

*LUNCHTIME SCHOOL SEWING CLUB

Love, your fabulous LSSC committee members (ELLA, ZOE AND AMMY)

Have to stop writing now, Diary, before my arm part falls off.

I will let you know EVERYTHING that happens about our LSSC meeting as soon as I get back from school tomorrow! I promise!

Yours 4 Ever,
Ella
XOXO

Tuesday, after school

Dear Diary,

The Good News

Zoe and Ammy and I got to school SUPER EARLY so we could put our posters up for the LSSC. ☺

The Bad News

We forgot to check with Ms Kahlo that we could use the Art and Craft Room first. ☹

So when we arrived there at 1.15 p.m. sharp, the room was already full of teensy-tiny Grade One students doing baby stuff for babies with paint.

The Badder News

Nobody turned up anyway. Not even ONE single person. ☹

NOOOOOOO!

The Good News

~~Forch~~ Fortunately, Ms Kahlo loved our idea about having a lunchtime sewing club. She told us we were all exceptionally creativerous and also HIGHLY inspirational. ☺☺☺

The ~~Gooder~~ Even Better News

Ms Kahlo said our idea was SO inspirational
we could DEFINITELY use the Art
and Craft Room for our sewing club at
lunchtime tomorrow. And also lots more
lunchtimes after that.

She even said she would
unlock the cupboard for us!
And help us set up the
sewing machines!

YESSSSSSSSSS!

Now all we have to do is go round to all our posters and change the day for our LSSC meeting on them.

(And also remind people in our class to read them.)

I CAN'T WAIT until tomorrow!

Ella
xOxO

Wednesday, after dinner

Dear Diary,

The Unbearably Sad Horrendously Horrible ~~Devostatingly~~ Devastatingly Bad News

Zoe and Ammy and I went to the Art and Craft Room again today at 1.15 p.m. sharp. Just like it said we would on our posters.

We waited . . .

and waited . . .

and waited . . .

but nobody turned up.

Again. 😞😞😞😞😞

Only joking!

Pazillions of people turned up!

Cordelia came. And Georgia. And also Poppy and Chloe and Daisy. And Fiona McTavish. And three girls called Sapphire and Sadie and Armani from one of the other Grade Five classes.

Princess Peach and Prinny and Jade stuck their heads in the door for about 3.1473 seconds to see what we were doing, wrinkled up their noses, then flounced off again.

Who even cares?

The first thing we did in the meeting was write down everyone's names in our special, official LSSC book. Zoe and Ammy and I had fun decorating the cover for it at morning recess.

Then I gave everyone a demonstration of how to make a stylish skirt out of a pillowcase and some elastic. And also some ricrac from Mum's Big Tin of Sewing Stuff. Nanna Kate gave me a special lesson on how to do it last night.

Everyone was AMAZED! Even Ms Kahlo.

And this is what my skirt looked like when it was finished!

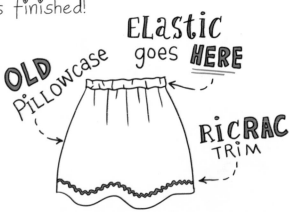

After that, we all had a nice chat about what everyone wants to make in our club.

Cordelia wants to make a new outfit for Mr Wombat.

Fiona wants to make a giganterous bag to keep her bagpipes in so they'll be easier to carry around.

Georgia wants to make a sweet little baby quilt for her sweet little baby brother.

Everyone else wants to make fantabulous
new clothes out of boring old stuff,
just like I did!

LSSC is funnerous fun! I can't wait until
our next meeting to find out what all our
new members bring in!

Talk later!

Ella
XOXO

Thursday, after school

Dear Diary,

I am soooo exciterated!

Guess what happened at lunchtime today!

You never will so I'll just tell you.

Pazillions more people turned up to our LSSC!!!

Sapphire and Sadie and Armani told the other girls in their class about how amazing and excellent and fantabulous our meeting was yesterday and some of them wanted to come too! And also a boy with aMAZing hair called Diesel.

Amazing Hair

Diesel

Ms Kahlo brought in a whole lot of extra crafty stuff to help us have fun with our fashion ideas.

IRON-ON SHAPES

PUFFY PaiNT

FaBRiC PENS

And guess what? My excellent teacher Ms Weiss came too. Ms Kahlo must have told her all about it in the teachers' staff room*. I am not even a tiny bit ~~serprised~~ surprised about this because Ms Weiss is one of the most stylishly stylish teachers I know.

MS WEISS

* A teachers' staff room is the place where teachers go to drink giganterous cups of coffee in between telling us importerant facts like how to spell trickerous words like 'pochemuchka'.**

Giganterous CUP OF COFFEE

✳✳ Pochemuchka is my new NEW favourite word. It means a person who asks too many questions.

Here are some of the things we made in LSSC today:

Daisy cut the back out of a giganterous pink T-shirt and glued some silver stars across the front of it. It looked just like a fantabulously fashionable dress! And she also cut the feet parts off some black and white stripy stockings to turn them into leggings!

FRONT   BACK
SILVER STARS
PINK T-SHIRT FABRIC
STRIPY LEGGINGS

Diesel brought in an old T-shirt too, only his was black. He slashed slashes across it and glued some gold musical notes around the edges. And he also made a stylish cape out of a piece of black cloth.

DIESEL

CAPE

SLASHES

GOLD MUSICAL NOTES

And you'll never guess what Georgia brought in, even if you kept having guesses for a pazillion bazillion gatrillion years!

An old leather jacket her aunty gave her! It's really, really, REALLY cool. She painted it bright red with silver racing stripes. Now it looks even cooler!

At the end of our meeting, everyone put their new outfits on and walked up and down the front of the Art and Craft Room like models in a fashion show.

And right at that exact same moment
I had a super-dupererous sensationally
BRILLIANT idea.

I can't tell you what it is yet though.

It's a SECRET. ☺☺☺

Yours 4 ever and ever,

Ella

xx

Friday, before dinner

Dearest Diary,

I'm really, really, really sorry, but I don't have enough time to write anything in you right now.

I'm too busy working on THE SECRET.

Love and kisses,
Ella

Saturday night, after dinner

Still too busy.

(Although there *may* have been a visit to an Op Shop✳ with Nanna Kate and some of the members of the LSSC today.

✳ An Op Shop is a shop full of old clothes and sweet little knick-knacks that people don't want any more.

We also went to one of those big stores where you can buy ▓▓▓▓▓▓▓▓

But I can't tell you anything more than that or it will give away **THE SECRET**.

E

Sunday night, before dinner

Still too busy.

Thursday, in bed, very, very, VERY late, so late I can barely stay awake long enough to write this

Dearest Diary,

I am really, really, really, REALLY sorry I haven't been able to write much this past week. My life has been TOTAL AND UTTER CHAOS!! But also FUNNEROUS FUN!

I will explain all tomorrow. I promise.

Talk soon!

Love,
Ella

X

Friday night, in bed, very late (again)

Dearest, darlingest Diary,

I can finally tell you what  is!

That's because we did it today.

Our LSSC had a fashion parade in the school hall at lunchtime!

It was called the Lunchtime School Sewing Club Fantabulous Fashion Parade.

Bazillions of students and teachers came. Even Mr Martini and Mrs Sneed (the main importerant teacher people at our school)!

And we showed off all the magnificently marvellous outfits we've been making in our LSSC all week. EsPECially the new ones we made after our TOP SECRET visit to the Op Shop on Saturday with Nanna Kate. ☺

Georgia

POPPY

SLeeves CUT OFF

RuFFLes aDDeD to SLeeVeS

HaND PainteD STRiPY LeatHeR Jacket

CROPPeD AT HEM

Decorative BOWS

POM POMS stitcHeD to SOCKS

Some of our LSSC members were a bit too quieterous and shy to model their outfits themselves. So Ammy and Zoe and I asked the other students in our class if they wanted to do it instead.

Peach and Prinny and Jade put their hands up straightaway!

And guess who were the besterest models?

If you said Peach and Prinny and Jade you are WRONG, WRONG, WRONG!

It was Peter and Raf!

Diesel made so many COOL OUTFITS there wasn't enough time for him to wear them all. So Peter and Raf helped him out.

RAF

PeTER

DiESEL

And Sadie from the other Grade Five class brought her totally aDORable little sister on stage wearing the sweet little outfit she made for her. ☺

Ms Kahlo and Ms Weiss (and also Mr Zugaro, my old teacher from last year) helped us to decorate the hall with lots of fashionably fashionable hall decorations. We spent ALL WEEK making them after school!

And Mrs Chang, our music teacher, played REALLY COOL MUSIC through the loud speakers for the models to walk up and down to.

At the end, all the models and sewing club members came out onto the stage and did a big bow.

And they gave Ammy and Zoe and me a GIGANTEROUS CLAP AND CHEER and also did foot stampering. And so did all the people sitting in the audience.

CHEER!

Woo-Hoo!

CLAP! CLAP!

YAY!

CHEER!

It was the absolutely, totally, completely besterest day of my life. Ever.

Good night, Diary.
Sleep tight. ☺

Your friend,
Ella
xOxOxO

PS (three days later)

Guess what happened at school today?

Mrs Danuzzo, who is the head of the School Disco organisering committee, called Zoe and Ammy and me up to the school office at lunchtime!

And she said she was sooooo impressed with our decorations for our LSSC Fantabulous Fashion Parade, she wants us all to be on the Disco Decorating Committee for next year's School Disco!

YAY!!!

She even wants us to help her choose the theme for next year!

DOUBLE YAY!!!

I've got a pazillion ideas already!

Hmmmm. Which one should I choose?

Ella

xxxx

Diaries

Read more of Ella's brilliant diary in

Double Dare You

Ballet Backflip

I ♥ Pets

Dreams come true

Christmas Chaos

Pony School Showdown

FRIENDS NOT FOREVER

WORST CAMP EVER

OPERATION Merry Christmas

FRIENDSHIP S.O.S

Going Green

TOTAL TV Drama

GOAL POWER

DIARY DISASTER

The Super Secret Club

GYM SQUAD TUMBLE

Time to Shine

Wildlife Rescue!

and look out for more coming soon!